For Melia and Mimi with love,
and with thanks to Dave and Dan
— J.M.

For Betty Wick
— W.W.

Library of Congress Cataloging-in-Publication Data.

Marzollo, Jean.

I spy I love you / by Jean Marzollo ; illustrated by Walter Wick.

p. cm. -- (Scholastic reader. Level 1)

ISBN 978-0-545-12513-0

1. Picture puzzles--Juvenile literature. 2. Love--Juvenile literature. I. Wick, Walter, ill. II. Title. III. Series.

GV1507.P47M293 2009

793.73--dc22

2009030022

ISBN-13: 978-0-545-12513-0
ISBN-10: 0-545-12513-8

10 9 8 7 6 5 4 3 2 1   9 10 11 12 13/0

Printed in the U.S.A. • First printing, December 2009

SCHOLASTIC READER
LEVEL 1
50-250 WORDS

I SPY

I LOVE YOU

Riddles by Jean Marzollo
Photographs by Walter Wick

Cartwheel
·B·O·O·K·S· ®

SCHOLASTIC INC.

New York   Toronto   London   Auckland
Sydney   Mexico City   New Delhi   Hong Kong

I spy

a heart,

 a yellow hat,

a fish,

 HOPE,

and a huggable cat.

I spy

a metal jet,

 a cart,

a dinosaur,

and an upside-down heart.

I spy

a spring,

 a little guitar,

a bride,

a groom,

and a red race car.

I spy

 a bridge,

a door in a tree,

 a red lantern,

and MOM & ME.

I spy

a ladder,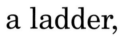

 a kangaroo,

BE MINE,

 a crown,

and a blue kazoo.

I spy

a comb,

a shoe on a bed,

a doll to love,

and a bow that's red.

I spy

a couple,

 a deer,

a horse,

and BE MY VALENTINE, of course

I spy

 a family,

the number 2,

 home plate,

and I WILL MARRY YOU.

I spy

a shovel,

a broom that's small,

a wooden heart,

 and a wooden ball.

I spy

a dolphin,

a sail that's blue,

an orange crayon,

and I LOVE YOU.

I spy two matching words.

 wooden heart

a dinosaur

 upside-down heart

I spy two matching words.

BE MINE

 BE MY VALENTINE

a bride

I spy two words that start with the letter H.

a groom

home plate

HOPE

I spy two words that start with the letters BR.

 bridge

bride

 a kangaroo

I spy two words that end with the letter R.

ladder

dinosaur

a blue kazoo

I spy two words that end with the letters LE.

 couple

a doll to love

 huggable cat

I spy two words that rhyme.

groom

 a deer

broom that's small

I spy three words that rhyme.

 shoe on a bed

blue kazoo

 a horse